For Dave, who has loved and supported me
through decades of ups, downs,
and in-betweens . . . xo
—S. D. R.

For my art teacher, Mr. Norris
—A. N. K.

Balzer + Bray is an imprint of HarperCollins Publishers.

Celebrate You!
Text copyright © 2019 by Sherri Duskey Rinker
Illustrations copyright © 2019 by A. N. Kang
All rights reserved. Manufactured in China.
No part of this book may be used or reproduced in any manner whatsoever without written permission except in the
case of brief quotations embodied in critical articles and reviews. For information address HarperCollins Children's Books,
a division of HarperCollins Publishers, 195 Broadway, New York, NY 10007.
www.harpercollinschildrens.com

ISBN 978-0-06-256402-3

The artist used charcoal, pencil, ink, and Adobe Photoshop to create the illustrations for this book.
Typography by Dana Fritts. Hand lettering by A. N. Kang.
19 20 21 22 23 SCP 10 9 8 7 6 5 4 3 2 1
❖
First Edition

By **Sherri Duskey Rinker**   Illustrations by **A. N. Kang**

Celebrate YOU!

BALZER + BRAY
An Imprint of HarperCollinsPublishers

On this special occasion,
we're just so filled with pride,
and we're thrilled, and we're grateful,
to be on your side!

So we'll pause for a moment
to look back, and ahead,
to say a few things about you
that just NEED to be said!

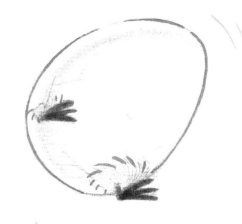

We're WOWED!

We're AMAZED

by all you can do,

and by all the challenges
you've gotten through. . . .

You're strong and
you're tough,
and yet
kindhearted, too.

Let's sing it; let's yell it! Let's celebrate **you!**

Strong will and hard work
have led you this way.
You've chased all your dreams . . .

Look where you are today!

We can hardly believe it—
you've just come so far.
We're amazed at what
a strong person you are!

First you crawled,
then you walked,

then you ran—
now you FLY!

Nothing can stop you
when you aim for the sky!

You were once very small,
but you grew and you grew.

You grew wise and you learned.
To yourself you've been true.

So today is the day—with a joyful *Hooray!*—
today is the day that we celebrate **you**!

CHEEEESE!

It hasn't always been easy,
but you land on your feet.

You have grit; you don't quit
or give in to defeat.
If you fumble or stumble,
you don't ever stop . . .

and you've remained humble
standing there at the top.

You can light up a room
with the smile on your face.

You're caring; you're kind.
You have wit; you have grace.

Best of all, you've kept your heart
in the right place!

Yet with all your success
and all that you've done,
you're still wonderfully you:
full of light, full of fun!

For all that you are
and all that you do,
we celebrate awesome,
UNSTOPPABLE you.

This is just the beginning.
Now go make your way.

Go shine in the world.
Make the most of each day.
Take every chance
to make more dreams come true.

You had better believe
that there's NOTHING
you can't do!

Loudly and proudly, we celebrate YOU!